INEQUITIES OF THE JUSTICE SYSTEM

Incarceration Issues:
Punishment, Reform, and Rehabilitation

TITLE LIST

INEQUITIES OF THE JUSTICE SYSTEM

by David Hunter

Mason Crest Publishers
Philadelphia

Mason Crest Publishers Inc.
370 Reed Road
Broomall, Pennsylvania 19008
(866) MCP-BOOK (toll free)

First printing
1 2 3 4 5 6 7 8 9 10

Library of Congress Cataloging-in-Publication Data

Hunter, David, 1974 June 16–
  Inequities of the justice system / by David Hunter.
     p. cm. — (Incarceration issues)
  Includes bibliographical references and index.
  ISBN 1-59084-995-7   ISBN 1-59084-984-1 (series)
  ISBN 978-1-59084-995-8   ISBN 978-1-59084-984-8 (series)

  1. Criminal Justice, Administration of—United States—Juvenile literature. 2. Discrimination in criminal justice administration—United States—Juvenile literature. I. Title. II. Series.
  HV9950.H85 2007
  364.973—dc22
                    2005032443

Interior design by MK Bassett-Harvey.
Interiors produced by Harding House Publishing Service, Inc.
www.hardinghousepages.com

Cover design by Peter Spires Culotta.

Printed in India by Quadra Press.

Contents

INTRODUCTION

by Larry E. Sullivan, Ph.D.

Prisons will be with us as long as we have social enemies. We will punish them for acts that we consider criminal, and we will confine them in institutions.

Prisons have a long history, one that fits very nicely in the religious context of sin, evil, guilt, and expiation. In fact, the motto of one of the first prison reform organizations was "Sin no more." Placing offenders in prison was, for most of the history of the prison, a ritual for redemption through incarceration; hence the language of punishment takes on a very theological cast. The word "penitentiary" itself comes from the religious concept of penance. When we discuss prisons, we are dealing not only with the law but with very strong emotions and reactions to acts that range from minor or misdemeanor crimes to major felonies like murder and rape.

Prisons also reflect the level of the civilizing process through which a culture travels, and it tells us much about how we treat our fellow human beings. The great nineteenth-century Russian author Fyodor Dostoyevsky, who was a political prisoner, remarked, "The degree of civilization in a society can be measured by observing its prisoners." Similarly, Winston Churchill, the great British prime minister during World War II, said that the "treatment of crime and criminals is one of the most unfailing tests of civilization of any country."

Since the very beginnings of the American Republic, we have attempted to improve and reform the way we imprison criminals. For much of the history of the American prison, we tried to rehabilitate or modify the criminal behavior of offenders through a variety of treatment programs. In the last quarter of the twentieth century, politicians and citizens alike realized that this attempt had failed, and we began passing stricter laws, imprisoning people for longer terms and building more prisons. This movement has taken a great toll on society. Approximately two million people are behind bars today. This movement has led to the

overcrowding of prisons, worse living conditions, fewer educational programs, and severe budgetary problems. There is also a significant social cost, since imprisonment splits families and contributes to a cycle of crime, violence, drug addiction, and poverty.

All these are reasons why this series on incarceration issues is extremely important for understanding the history and culture of the United States. Readers will learn all facets of punishment: its history; the attempts to rehabilitate offenders; the increasing number of women and juveniles in prison; the inequality of sentencing among the races; attempts to find alternatives to incarceration; the high cost, both economically and morally, of imprisonment; and other equally important issues. These books teach us the importance of understanding that the prison system affects more people in the United States than any institution, other than our schools.

7

CHAPTER 1

LAW AND ORDER

"In the criminal justice system, the people are represented by two separate yet equally important groups: the police, who investigate crime; and the district attorneys, who prosecute the offenders. These are their stories."

—introductory narration for *Law & Order*

The law has long fascinated people from many different walks of life on many different levels. The multitude of television shows made about the law, law enforcement, and judicial affairs makes this readily apparent. Most of these shows focus on the drama of the courtroom and on the stories of people whose lives have been changed in court. While some shows and films about the law are based on factual events, most are purely fictional, made solely for entertainment.

Some people prefer a more academic approach to law on television, however. Until recently, these people had to satisfy themselves with the occasional documentary exploring certain high-profile legal cases or examining some aspect of the judicial system itself. With the boom in cable television networks in the 1990s, however, this changed. Now, cable networks such as C-SPAN and Court TV provide nearly twenty-four-hour coverage of legislative and legal proceedings, and shows like Cops provide people with an exciting glimpse into the work of crime fighters.

So what about the law attracts so many people? Perhaps it is because, like a good novel, the pursuit of justice is filled with conflict and suspense. On the streets, police officers chase down notorious felons and search for crucial pieces of evidence. Defense attorneys and prosecutors engage in carefully *choreographed* battles for justice—like *gladiators* who use words and evidence as their weapons—while the fate of the accused hangs in the balance.

In real life, police work is rarely so thrilling as portrayed on television, and legal proceedings are not so exciting as a hockey game or a tennis match. Instead of resembling a sporting event, the most dramatic court cases might play out more like a very slow chess match—the lawyers planning their questions, statements, and witnesses carefully over the course of many days or weeks. And that's just the most dramatic cases. The majority of cases brought to court are resolved with little fanfare and a minimum of conflict.

In fact, it's probably a good thing that police officers aren't chasing down criminals every minute of their day. If they did, they wouldn't have time to help stranded motorists or write traffic citations. In the same vein, it's fortunate that court cases don't resemble sporting events. Judges and juries are instructed to remain emotionally unattached to the cases they hear. This is to prevent people's emotions from clouding their judgment. It would be difficult to remain objective if cheerleaders and fans were in the court rooting for their favorite lawyer.

Defense attorneys are just one of the combatants in the battle for justice.

Police may use computers to help them gather evidence.

But even if the reality is less exciting than the television shows, people are still drawn to shows about law because they have an inborn desire to see the good guys win and the bad guys lose. When we watch a movie, we usually want to see the hero save the day. In fact, most movies end like that because movie producers know that people want a happy ending. Police work and court cases are not scripted or written out in advance the way movies are. Unfortunately, the good guys sometimes lose, and the bad guys sometimes win.

When that happens in legal settings, it can create quite a controversy. Sometimes, the wrong people are arrested, while the true criminals go free. In courts, the innocent are sometimes wrongfully convicted or held responsible for a crime. Other times, people who are guilty of a crime are wrongfully acquitted, or declared not guilty. All of these are examples of inequities in the justice system. An inequity is something that is unfair or unjust. Another type of inequity in the courts might involve a person who is punished far more severely than her actions dictate.

THE PEOPLE WHO UPHOLD THE LAW

As the opening lines to the popular television drama *Law & Order* indicate, there is more than one group appointed to uphold the law. In this book we look at three of those groups: law enforcement, the judiciary system, and correctional services. Law enforcement includes the police and other agencies that work to ensure people are obeying the law. The judiciary system is comprised of the various courts that interpret the law and judge whether people are guilty or innocent of crimes. Correctional services are the institutions in which people convicted of crimes are punished and rehabilitated, or helped to become better citizens.

Although shows such as *Law & Order* are fictional, many of them attempt to portray the legal system accurately. Clearly, these shows take some liberties for the sake of drama, because television viewers want to see an exciting show. However, many of these shows are thoroughly researched and written in conjunction with legal professionals who act as advisers to make the shows as realistic as possible. For this reason, *Law & Order* serves as a good example of how the justice system works.

If you ever watch *Law & Order*, you will see that, in general, the police or some other law enforcement agency investigates a crime. Their duty in this regard is to try to collect as much evidence about a crime as they possibly can. This information may take the form of testimony from witnesses, fingerprints, **DNA samples** from hair or blood, security camera footage, or a host of other things that help to indicate who might have committed the crime. When the police have collected all the evidence they can find, they decide whether they want to charge a suspect with the crime.

Many times, there is not enough evidence to charge someone with a crime. This is often the situation in cases of theft. For example, a person might not realize somebody has stolen his wallet until it is too late to determine who stole it. In these circumstances, the case is left open. If more information is later found pertaining to that case, the police can add the information to the file and continue their investigation.

It's a judge's job to help determine the consequences of breaking the law.

THE LAW IN FICTION

Many television shows, movies, and books focus on some aspect of the law. Here are some examples, from the 1960s to today:

Film: *To Kill a Mockingbird, 12 Angry Men, Legal Eagles, A Few Good Men, LA Confidential, A Time to Kill, Shawshank Redemption*

Television: *Perry Mason, Dragnet, Arrest and Trial, Matlock, Hill Street Blues, NYPD Blue, Law & Order*

Authors: Scott Turow, John Grisham, James Patterson

Sometimes, however, the police are able to gather a great deal of information. They use this information to determine who to charge with a crime. They then arrest that person and turn the case over to the judiciary. It is the judiciary's job to try to determine whether the person who is charged with a crime actually committed it, and to determine the consequences of breaking the law.

Many factors determine how a court will deal with a legal case. The age of the person accused of committing the crime, the type of crime committed, where it was committed, the severity of the crime, and many other factors are important considerations when determining what type of court will hear the case. These same factors also determine many other things, including whether a judge alone or a jury will decide the trial and where the trial will be held.

In this book, we focus primarily on criminal courts, but even among criminal courts, there are differences in procedure. There are also many

similarities. In general, a judge presides over, or supervises, a trial. The person accused of committing a crime, called the defendant, is given the opportunity to try to demonstrate her innocence, usually with the help of a defense lawyer. On the other hand, the **_prosecuting_** attorneys try to prove the defendant is guilty of the crime. After the defense and the prosecution have presented their cases, the jury must weigh all the information they have heard. Then they must decide whether to convict the defendant, which means they find her guilty, or to acquit the defendant, which means they find her innocent.

Depending on the severity of the crime and the amount of information presented by the defense and the prosecution, a trial could take as little as a few minutes to as long as several months. If the jury decides the defendant is guilty, then—depending on where the trial takes place—they may make a suggestion to the judge regarding the defendant's sentence, or punishment. Except for the death sentence (which in a Supreme Court ruling must be decided by a jury), in general, it is the judge who actually

A court of law is a place where people's rights are protected.

TYPES OF COURTS

There are many different types of courts. Different courts hear different types of cases or handle different classes of people. Some examples include:

- Juvenile or Family Court: Handles cases involving young people not yet old enough to be tried as adults.
- Criminal Court: Deals with cases in which an adult has violated a law. Criminal courts can punish people with a wide variety of sanctions, including community service, monetary fines, and time in prison.
- Civil Court: Deals with cases that do not involve broken laws. Often, civil trials involve one person trying to get compensation for damage from another person.
- Appeals or Appellate Court: A court with authority to change the decision of a lower court. If a person loses a case in one court, he may be able to appeal it, or take it to an appeals court.

decides the sentence. In many cases, the consequences of breaking the law include serving time in prison, though this is not always the case.

At any rate, after a person is convicted of a crime by a court, he is turned over to correctional services. This component of the justice system is responsible for punishing, and in some instances rehabilitating, a person convicted of a crime. This often involves time in prison. In some instances, however, the judge or jury might be satisfied with counseling, education, or a monetary fine.

While the specific procedures and details of all this may seem very complicated—and they certainly are—the purpose of the judicial system is really quite simple. The judicial system is in place to help protect people and to safeguard individuals' rights and interests.

Sometimes, courts of law promote injustice rather than justice.

JUDICIAL DEFINITIONS

Many of the words in this book are usually only used when talking about judicial matters. Here are some brief definitions that you can refer to if you need clarification.

Defendant: In a criminal trial, the person accused of a crime.

Prosecution: The lawyers representing the government. Their job is to try to prove the defendant guilty.

Jury: A group of between twelve and twenty-four people who listen to the facts of a case and decide whether the defendant is innocent or guilty.

Convict: To find guilty.

Acquit: To find not guilty.

Sentence: The punishment given by a judge to the defendant if found guilty.

HUMAN IMPERFECTION

In most cases in North America, judicial systems do quite well in fulfilling their purpose. That is to say, they are usually fair and accurate. Unfortunately, nobody is perfect, and human beings run all three components of the judicial system—law enforcement, the judiciary, and correctional services. Thus, none of these components is perfect either. Sometimes, the very institutions we have in place to promote justice actually produce injustice. In this book, we look at some of the ways that inequities are caused in the justice system. Hopefully, by better understanding how these inequities are caused, we can explore better and more just alternatives.

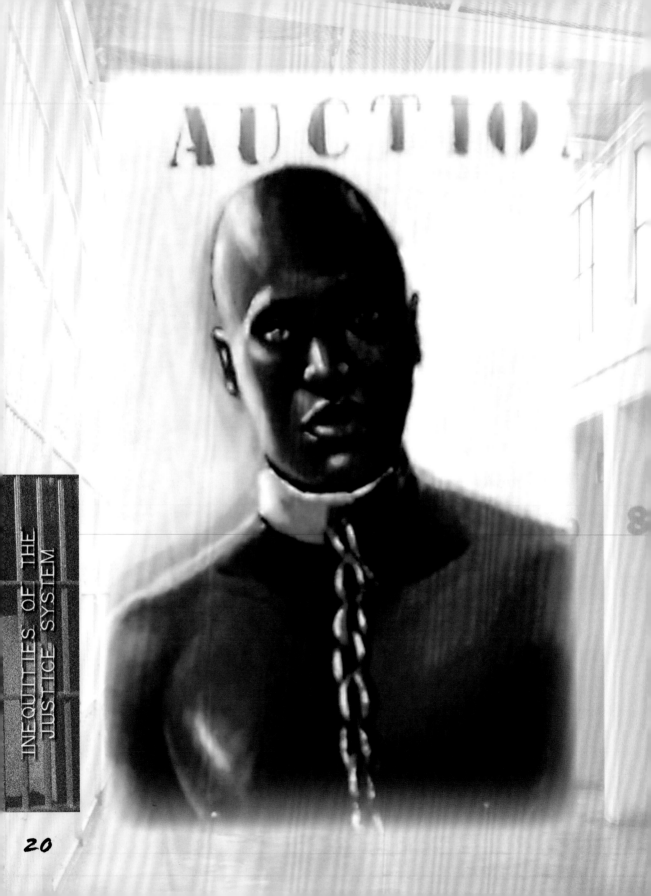

CHAPTER 2

Is Justice Truly (Color) Blind?

"Until justice is blind to color, until education is unaware of race, until opportunity is unconcerned with the color of men's skins, emancipation will be a proclamation but not a fact."
—Lyndon B. Johnson, Memorial Day 1963

Rubin Carter was a middleweight boxer whose power and aggressive boxing style won him the nickname "Hurricane." He was exciting to watch and quickly became a favorite of many fans. In his first twenty-four matches, he won twenty and lost only four, scoring thirteen knockouts. His victories gained him the rank of number-three contender to the middleweight title.

In 1964, he got his chance at the title in a bout against champion Joey Giardello. After a grueling fifteen-round fight, the ringside judges awarded Giardello victory in a unanimous decision. It was the closest Rubin "Hurricane" Carter would come to the title.

After his match with Giardello, Carter's performance dropped considerably. In his next fifteen matches, he won seven, lost seven, and had one *draw*. By 1966, he was no longer even ranked in the top ten. What's more, Carter fell afoul of the law. Although no charges were ever filed, Carter had allegedly been involved in a fight in a hotel in London, England. The former contender had fallen to new lows.

He would fall further yet. On June 17, 1966, three people were killed and another shot in the head when two men entered the Lafayette Bar and Grill in Paterson, New Jersey, and started shooting. On May 26, 1967, Carter and his friend John Artis were found guilty of murder and sentenced to life in prison.

Carter was not new to prison. In fact, he had developed quite a long record of troublesome behavior long before becoming a boxer. At the age of fourteen, he had been sentenced to a juvenile *reformatory* for assault and robbery charges. He escaped from the reformatory and entered the army, but was *court-martialed* four times and discharged because he was an undisciplined soldier. Immediately after returning to civilian life, he was arrested for escaping from the juvenile reformatory and was sentenced to a year in prison. Shortly after his release from prison in 1957, Carter was convicted of robbing and beating several people, and went back to prison for four more years until 1961. Because of his long criminal record, many people believed he had committed the murders in 1966.

After his 1967 conviction, however, Carter vehemently maintained that he was innocent, that he was not involved in the shootings. His supporters contended there were many errors in the way the investigation and the trial were conducted. Some people said the investigators were biased and that the witnesses were not telling the truth. One of the strongest arguments Carter's lawyers made was that the jury that decided his fate was comprised solely of white people.

Rubin Carter is black.

Rubin "Hurricane" Carter

The objections of Carter's lawyers were strong enough to gain him a retrial in 1976, nine years after going to prison. This time, a racially mixed jury heard the case. Although the testimony of one of the witnesses was questionable, the court once again ruled against Carter, sending him back to prison.

Carter, his lawyers, and his supporters in Canada and the United States continued the struggle to free him from prison. Celebrities such as Muhammad Ali and Joan Baez lent their presence and their voice to the effort. Bob Dylan wrote a song called "Hurricane," in which he expressed the view that Carter was innocent. New evidence continued to surface,

Rubin "Hurricane" Carter in prison

but New Jersey state prosecutors delayed in responding to the evidence. In 1985, Carter and his lawyers finally won a third trial, this time in the U.S. District Court under Judge H. Lee Sarokin.

After producing several hundred pages of reasoning why the original sentences had been unfair, the defense team presented their arguments. The prosecutors responded to those arguments. After hearing all these arguments and responses, Judge Sarokin ruled that the previous two trials had been conducted improperly and that Rubin Carter be freed from prison.

In his judgment, which was itself seventy pages long, Judge Sarokin wrote that in the original two trials, "the jury was permitted to draw inferences of guilt based solely upon the race of the petitioners (Carter and Artis), but yet was denied information that might have supported their claims of innocence." In essence, the judge ruled that the first two trials were determined not by the facts of the case, but by the biases—or preconceived opinions—of the police who investigated the murders and the lawyers who prosecuted the case.

After nearly twenty years in prison, Carter finally had his freedom. He was never officially exonerated, or cleared, however, of the charges brought against him. Rather, the state of New Jersey opted not to bring him to trial a third time because of the cost and time required to do so. In the U.S. justice system, a person is considered innocent until proven guilty in court. Without a third trial, Carter is now living in Canada, legally innocent of the crimes.

The story of Rubin "Hurricane" Carter is very controversial and filled with uncertainty. Did Rubin Carter and John Artis murder three people in the Lafayette Bar and Grill in June 1966? It may be only they know the answer to that question. It points, however, to one of the weaknesses of the judicial system—bias.

SOCIETY'S INEQUITIES

Many of the inequities **inherent** in the current judicial system reflect inequities that exist in society as a whole. People often make assumptions

Bob Dylan is shown here visiting Hurricane Carter in prison.

and form opinions about a person based solely on some aspect of that person's identity. These ideas are often called stereotypes. A stereotype is an oversimplified characterization that is applied to some group of people without considering individual differences between people in that group. For example, somebody might say New Yorkers are unfriendly. However, many people from New York are quite friendly. Thus, this statement stereotypes New Yorkers unfairly.

When people use stereotypes like this as the basis of their decisions or their behavior toward other people, this is often called discrimination. Discrimination can occur in any situation in which people make judgments and decisions about people who are different from them. People can discriminate against other people on the basis of many identifying features, including age, race, gender, and sexual orientation. This chapter focuses on racial discrimination in the justice system, the practice of treating people unfairly and unequally because of their race, their ethnicity, or the color of their skin.

BIAS AND DISCRIMINATION

Everyone has biases. A bias is just a preference. For example, if you have a bias for the color blue, then you prefer blue. However, jurors with very strong biases that might interfere with their ability to make a fair decision are dismissed from the jury.

Discrimination involves more than simply preferring something. When a person discriminates against someone, it means that he acts unfairly toward that person. For example, a juror who makes a decision based on the color of a defendant's skin rather than based on the facts of a case is discriminating against the defendant.

RACIAL DISCRIMINATION

Until the middle of the twentieth century, racial discrimination was tragically common and obvious in North American courts of law. Since the early nineteenth century, both Canada and the United States accepted floods of immigrants from Europe, Asia, and Central and South America. All too often, however, the welcome extended to these newcomers was anything but warm.

Often, already established citizens of North America felt the new immigrants were taking their jobs and threatening their culture. This led to resentment and conflict in many areas, which itself led to discrimination in schools, industries, and in the courts. Inequities in the justice system

A slave market in New Orleans in the early 1800s; slavery left an indelible mark on North Americans' attitudes and memories.

were particularly common in the American South, where the legacies of the **slave economy** still influenced people's attitudes and memories. Even in the northern states and Canada, however, minorities suffered grave injustices at the hands of intolerant white people.

THE DULUTH LYNCHINGS

On June 14, 1920, the John Robinson Circus was preparing to leave the city of Duluth, Minnesota, after having performed there. A young woman named Irene Tusken and her friend John Sullivan were walking around the circus grounds watching the workers pack up their equipment to leave. Sullivan went to work later that night while Miss Tusken returned to her parents' home and went to bed. Nothing seemed amiss that evening. Neither Mr. Sullivan nor Miss Tusken appeared overly distressed about anything, and neither mentioned anything to indicate that something bad had happened. The next day, however, John Sullivan reported to his father that several African American employees of the circus had held him at gunpoint and had raped Miss Tusken.

Early the morning of June 15, police arrested six African American circus laborers for the rape of Miss Tusken. Later that day, however, Miss Tusken's doctor examined her and found no signs of assault or rape. Aside from Miss Tusken and John Sullivan's testimony, police found no evidence of wrongdoing by the circus workers. Nevertheless, the six men were arrested and taken to the Duluth city jail to await trial. Sadly, several of them would never have the chance to be defended in court.

A local newspaper ran a story about the reported rape on the same day police arrested the six men. Enraged by the story, a mob of over one thousand white people formed outside the jail. The police, outnumbered and ordered not to use their guns, did little as the mob broke through windows and doors into the jail and pulled the six African American men out onto the street.

The mob conducted a fake trial of the men and pronounced three of them—Elias Clayton, Elmer Jackson, and Isaac McGhie—guilty. The white mob came to this conclusion based not on evidence or testimony as a real court would, but based solely on the fact that the circus workers were African American. The mob then beat the three men and hanged them from a nearby lamppost, killing them.

The next day, the Minnesota National Guard arrived in Duluth to keep the peace. On June 17, the Duluth District Court began holding trials of the men who were involved in the incident. Two African American men from the circus were tried for rape. Although there was little evidence to support it, one man—Max Mason—was convicted and sentenced to prison for seven to thirty years. He was released from prison after four years under the condition that he leave Minnesota.

IS JUSTICE TRULY (COLOR) BLIND?

> :::
>
> The lynching in Duluth will have a wholesome effect on the class of help carried by ordinary circus and the carnival troupes. The chances are that no colored help with a carnival attraction or circus in the county will be tolerated hereafter.
>
> :::

A 1920 newspaper editorial claimed that the Duluth lynchings would have a "wholesome effect."

In the aftermath of the *lynching* and rioting, eight white men who had taken part in the mob were tried for rioting and for murder. Three of them—Louis Dondino, Gilbert Henry Stephenson, and Carl John Alfred Hammerberg—were convicted of rioting. They were sentenced to serve up to five years in prison, but were all released after only one year. Nobody was convicted of murder.

Clearly, the Duluth lynchings show racism and discrimination in the most overt—or obvious and direct—way. Despite a lack of evidence and very questionable testimony, Max Mason was sentenced to prison for a longer period of time than three of the men who may have been involved in killing Elias Clayton, Elmer Jackson, and Isaac McGhie.

LEGAL DISCRIMINATION

Unlike the Duluth lynchings, most instances of racial discrimination in courts of law are not so obvious. In many cases, judges and lawyers use

The Duluth jail, after rioters knocked out windows and broke through the doors

standard court procedures—the very same procedures that are designed to make trials fair and unbiased—to make a trial unfair for minority defendants.

One of the most common ways that unjust legal systems do this is by selecting a jury that will be biased against minority defendants. A jury biased in this manner will decide against minority defendants more often than an unbiased jury, which results in more convictions and longer prison sentences for minority defendants. At one time in some parts of the American South, African Americans were systematically excluded from jury rosters. Courts did this in a variety of ways that made it appear as though they were selecting juries randomly and objectively.

In 1879, in the landmark case *Strauder v. West Virginia*, the U.S. Supreme Court ruled that it was unconstitutional to restrict jury selection lists to white men. The Court held that such restrictions violated the Fourteenth Amendment to the Constitution, which guarantees equal protection under the law to all citizens.

Despite the Supreme Court's decision, courts, particularly in the American South, continued to exclude minorities, and especially Afri-

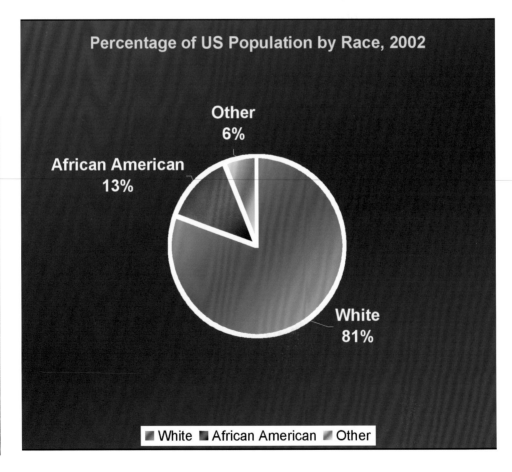

Percentage of US Population by Race, 2002

Other
6%

African American
13%

White
81%

White African American Other

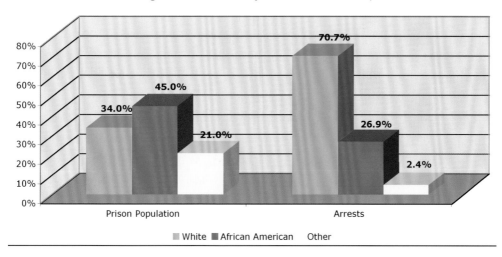

Percentage of US Prison Population and Arrests, 2002

Prison Population — White 34.0%, African American 45.0%, Other 21.0%

Arrests — White 70.7%, African American 26.9%, Other 2.4%

White ■ African American ■ Other

can Americans, from jury duty. Only a few years later in Delaware, for example, African American jurors were systematically dismissed under the pretense of being unqualified for jury duty. As late as the 1940s in Georgia, the names of potential jurors were written on cards that were colored differently depending on the juror's race or ethnicity. The names of white jurors were written on white cards, while the names of minority jurors were written on colored cards. Not surprisingly, when court officials "randomly" drew cards to choose jurors for a trial, only white cards were typically drawn.

Over the years, much has been done to help promote equal and just treatment of minorities in courts. That struggle continues to this day, waged in the courtroom, in the legislative halls of government, and in the minds and attitudes of people everywhere. However, the racial inequities in the criminal justice system do not stem only from the courts.

POLICE DISCRIMINATION

According to the FBI's Uniform Crime Report (UCR), a program that records the crime reports from police agencies all around the country,

African American offenders constituted about 27 percent of all arrests in the United States in 2002. For violent crimes—such as murder and robbery—the African American arrest rate was even higher at 38 percent of all arrests. On the other hand, white people constituted about 71 percent of all arrests and 60 percent of all violent crime arrests.

In other words, white people were arrested much more frequently than African American people. Numbers like that can be misleading, though. According to the American census, African Americans made up only 13 percent of the total U.S. population in 2002. White people made up fully 80 percent. As we take a look back at the crime statistics once more, we can see that African American people are extremely overrepresented in criminal arrests. That is to say, African Americans are arrested far more than their representation in the population would dictate.

Worst of all, African Americans constituted 50 percent of all murder arrests and 54 percent of all robbery arrests. These statistics in particular are very disturbing. Although African Americans make up only 13 percent of the American population, they make up half of all arrests for murder and over half of all arrests for robbery. However, these numbers alone do not tell the whole story.

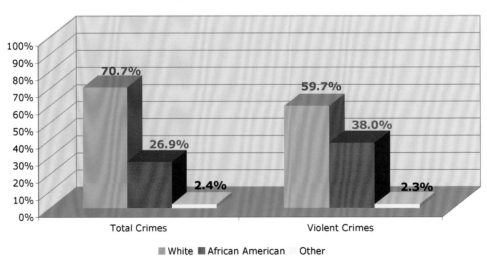

Percentage of US Arrests by Race, 2002

Percentage of US Murder and Robbery Arrests by Race, 2002

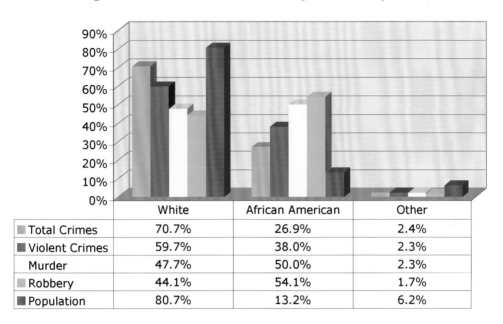

	White	African American	Other
Total Crimes	70.7%	26.9%	2.4%
Violent Crimes	59.7%	38.0%	2.3%
Murder	47.7%	50.0%	2.3%
Robbery	44.1%	54.1%	1.7%
Population	80.7%	13.2%	6.2%

Arrests and Perceptions of African Americans, 2002

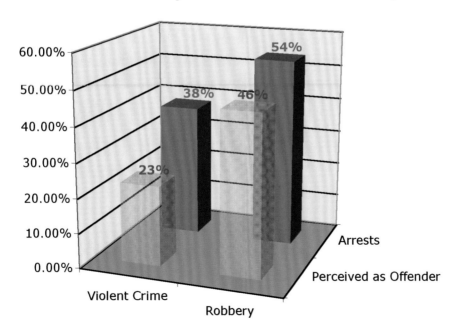

IS JUSTICE TRULY (COLOR) BLIND?

35

The Duluth police force in 1920

Another tool for analyzing crime statistics, called the National Crime Victimization Survey (NCVS), surveys approximately 160,000 people each year to estimate crime statistics and determine characteristics about both victims of crime and criminal offenders. By surveying a large, random sampling of people, the NCVS arrives at crime statistics through the eyes of crime victims. According to the NCVS, victims of violent crime perceived the offender to be African American in about 23 percent of all violent crimes. Robbery victims perceived their attackers to be African American in approximately 46 percent of robbery cases.

Let's compare these numbers. Robbery victims perceived their attackers to be African American in 46 percent of robbery cases. On the other hand, African Americans constitute 54 percent of robbery arrests. Think about that. Forty-six out of every one hundred people who are robbed say that the robber was African American. Yet fifty-four out of every one hundred people arrested for robbery are African American. That

COMPARING THE NCVS AND THE UCR

Although it is very useful and instructive to compare the NCVS and the UCR, there are some problems in doing so. For one, the NCVS deals with victims' perceptions, which may be incorrect. A person who is robbed may not get a good look at his attacker, and thus report the attacker's race incorrectly. Also, the UCR reports arrests, but arrests do not always result in convictions. Some people who are arrested are found not guilty in court. While both reports are useful, neither is guaranteed to be completely accurate.

difference could indicate that police officers are arresting too many African Americans, and possibly many who are innocent.

RACE AND PRISON POPULATIONS

The disparity between whites and African Americans becomes even more pronounced when you look at prison populations. According to the Bureau of Justice Statistics Bulletin, in 2002, African Americans constituted over 45 percent of the total prison population. Whites—who make up a much larger percentage of the population of the country—made up only 34 percent of the prison population. How is it that African

Is lady justice ever really color blind?

Americans can account for only 27 percent of the arrests in 2002, but 45 percent of the prison population?

In fact, there are several ways to explain this. For one, African Americans are arrested for a larger percentage of violent crime arrests than are whites. Violent crimes are more likely to result in a prison sentence than are many nonviolent crimes. In addition, violent crimes usually carry a much longer prison sentence than nonviolent crimes. Thus, on average, whites do not stay in prison as long. In fact, for some less serious crimes, offenders—regardless of their race—might be sent to more temporary facilities such as jails rather than to prison. Because whites are arrested for a greater percentage of nonviolent crimes, the total number of whites in prison at any given time will likely be lower.

But do these factors adequately explain the huge difference between the number of whites and African Americans in prison? Unfortunately, there's really no way to know for sure. What we do know is that historically, minorities have received unfair treatment under the law. Although the discrimination and bias that were so tragically illustrated in cases like the Duluth lynchings are no longer as obvious or as damaging, they are undoubtedly still a factor in both police arrests and criminal trials.

For some people, proving that discrimination is a factor in court often makes the difference between incarceration and freedom. Proving that is often a difficult task, unfortunately, because many of the questions that need to be asked to identify discrimination don't have simple answers. Numbers and percentages, for example, don't tell the whole story, and it can sometimes be difficult to recognize people's biases. Nevertheless, the struggle for justice is one worth fighting.

CHAPTER 3

THE COST OF JUSTICE

"Money frees you from doing things you dislike. Since I dislike doing nearly everything, money is handy."
—Groucho Marx, comedian

In 1961, a poor electrician from Florida named Clarence Earl Gideon entered the law books and helped rewrite the way that criminal cases are conducted in American courts. Gideon had been arrested and brought to trial for breaking into a pool hall and stealing a small amount of money and some drinks. Unable to afford a lawyer, he asked the court in which he was

being tried to provide him with a public defender. His request was denied, and he had to act as his own defense lawyer during his trial.

He lost.

From prison, Gideon wrote to the U.S. Supreme Court to ask for an appeal of the original decision. In 1963, the Supreme Court agreed to hear the appeal. In *Gideon v. Wainwright*, the Supreme Court ruled unanimously that Gideon's right to equal treatment under the law was denied in his original trial. The justices of the Supreme Court argued that, due to the complexities of the law, a person could not possibly defend himself adequately in court without a lawyer. The case set a **precedent** in the American criminal justice system. From that point on, all criminal courts were required to appoint a lawyer for those people who could not afford to hire one.

The ruling sent shockwaves through the prisons of Florida and other states. In Florida alone, several thousand inmates were released from prison as a result of the decision. Clarence Earl Gideon, ironically, was not released. He was granted a second trial, however. In his retrial, his lawyer helped to prove his innocence, and he was cleared of all charges.

PUBLIC DEFENDERS

Before *Gideon v. Wainwright*, the number of public defenders—lawyers who defend people who can't afford their own lawyer—was extremely low. In 1951, only seven public defender organizations existed in the United States. After 1963, however, that number ballooned rapidly. Today, the public defender system helps give legal representation to many people who otherwise would have none, giving them an opportunity to prove their innocence in court.

Unfortunately, the system is not perfect. For one thing, public defenders and court-appointed attorneys are paid less for their services than private lawyers. Often, public defenders are inexperienced. Many of them are recent graduates who have never actually tried a case, working in programs that help reduce their student loan debt. In addition, many

Clarence Earl Gideon was eventually cleared of all charges.

public defenders are tremendously overworked, with caseloads that are far too large and resources and time that are stretched far too thin.

In their 1995 article "Judges and the Politics of Death," Stephen Bright and Patrick Keenan argue that many judges fail to uphold people's constitutionally guaranteed right to equal treatment under the law by appointing lawyers who are ***apathetic***, who simply don't care about the outcome of their cases. Bright and Keenan illustrate their point with many examples, such as that of a court-appointed attorney "who occasionally falls asleep in court, and is known primarily for hurrying through capital trials like 'greased lightning' without much questioning or making objections." They then go on to state that ten of that lawyer's clients have received death sentences—not a statistic to be proud of.

Bright and Keenan also argue that the lawyers appointed to a defendant are often unqualified or inexperienced. They illustrate this with the example of a lawyer only a few months out of law school, who had never even studied criminal law, appointed to defend a person in a capital case. Another example is the court-appointed lawyer who told the judge that he didn't know what he was doing.

Clearly, these examples don't inspire the public's confidence in court-appointed lawyers or public defenders. Much research has been done on the effectiveness of public defenders compared to private attorneys. Most of these studies find that defendants who have their own lawyer are less likely to be sentenced to prison than people with a court-appointed attorney. In addition, convicted offenders with a private attorney generally serve shorter sentences than those with court-appointed attorneys.

There are many possible reasons for this disparity—a difference that can be explained through legitimate factors. It might be true that public defenders are less effective than private attorneys. On the other hand, it may be the case that, in general, people who have their own attorneys are put on trial for less serious crimes, and so are incarcerated less frequently and for shorter periods of time. Perhaps the statistics are **skewed** because people who can afford their own lawyers tend not to engage in serious crimes such as robbery, theft, or murder.

Still, it is clear that people who rely on public defenders in court are more likely to go to prison and are more likely to get a longer sentence. Conversely, people who are wealthy enough to hire a private attorney are less likely to be convicted and sentenced to prison. That isn't to say that wealthy people are never found guilty of crimes, but they are found guilty far less frequently than poor people. Looking at the prison population in Canada confirms this: more than 70 percent of Canadian prison inmates have an unstable work history. In other words, a large majority of the people in Canadian prisons have a history of being either unemployed or unable to hold a job for an extended time. The same holds true for American prisons.

A court-appointed lawyer may have less experience than a private attorney.

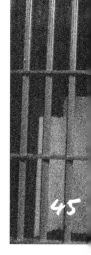

The amount of money you have may influence the type of justice you receive.

MONEY AND JUSTICE

It seems likely that money and social standing have a role in courts and in the criminal justice system in general. This can be partially explained by recognizing a disparity between the wealthy and the poor. For instance, one might argue that people without jobs are more likely to steal than are people who have steady paychecks. After all, if you can pay for something, why risk getting in trouble by stealing it? An important question to ask, though, is how much of that difference is a result of economic disparities, and how much is a result of discrimination.

Socioeconomic discrimination is the practice of treating people unfairly because of their place in society. The amount of money a person has, the sort of neighborhood where a person lives, the job a person

CAPITAL CASES

In criminal courts, a capital case or trial is an extremely serious trial. While other trials may end with the defendant going to prison, a capital case can result in the death sentence. The death penalty itself is often referred to as "capital punishment."

works—all of these are factors in socioeconomic discrimination. More so than racial discrimination in the courts, socioeconomic discrimination can work in two directions. Not only do people who are poor suffer from ineffective legal counsel and have a greater chance of being convicted in court, but people who are rich and famous generally have better lawyers and often tend to benefit from their status.

Take the case of Martha Stewart, for example. Martha Stewart made a name for herself as one of the premier guides to home life, gardening, cooking, and etiquette. Her work in magazines and on television made her both popular and wealthy. On December 27, 2001, she sold 3,928 shares of stock in ImClone Systems, a company founded by her friend, Samuel Waksal. The next day, the United States Food and Drug Administration announced that it would not approve a new medicine that ImClone had developed. The price of ImClone stock dropped rapidly. By selling her stock when she did, Martha Stewart avoided losing approximately forty-five thousand dollars.

The United States Securities and Exchange Commission, a government agency that oversees the stock market and investigates financial

Arrests for blue-collar crimes are far more common than for white-collar crimes.

wrongdoing, claimed that Stewart had been involved in "insider trading"—using information that most stockholders did not have to profit unfairly from the sale of her ImClone stock. Insider trading is illegal, and so Martha Stewart found herself in court.

On March 5, 2005, Stewart was found guilty of conspiracy, obstruction of justice, and two counts of making false statements about the sale of her ImClone stock. Stewart received five months in prison, followed by five months of confinement in her home, and two years of probation. Plus, she was fined thirty thousand dollars for her misdeeds. Some people believed her sentence was too lenient. Usually, the charges that she faced carry a maximum sentence of twenty years in prison.

WHITE-COLLAR VS. BLUE-COLLAR CRIMES

Crime of this nature, against companies and large organizations, is often called "white-collar" crime. The term refers to the traditional white, button-down shirts worn by people in high-paying professional careers, such as doctors, lawyers, bankers, and administrators. White-collar crimes include insider trading, embezzlement, *fraud*, computer crime, and forgery.

In contrast to white-collar crime is what is known as "blue-collar" crime. These are the more common sorts of crimes, including larceny-theft, automobile theft, robbery, burglary, and acts of violence. Blue-collar crimes are far more common than their white-collar counterparts. In 2002, for example, the FBI reported over 840,000 arrests in the United States for larceny-theft. By comparison, only slightly more than 13,000 arrests were made for embezzlement.

These numbers can be misleading, however. In 2002, seven million Americans reported being the victims of larceny-theft, for a total loss of 4.9 billion dollars. That is an average of seven hundred dollars lost for each reported instance of larceny-theft.

The United States Chamber of Commerce, on the other hand, estimates that embezzlement costs American companies and organizations
upward of fifty billion dollars every year. That's seven times more money
lost due to white-collar crime than is lost due to blue-collar crime.

Larceny-theft is generally a crime against a single person or place of
business. For example, a girl who steals CDs from a music store or a boy
who has taken five dollars from somebody's school locker has committed larceny-theft. In these cases, it would seem that only one individual
person or store is affected by the theft. In embezzlement cases, that loss
is felt by an entire business or organization. For example, an accountant
who embezzles money from his company would apparently hurt only
that company.

These crimes seem to only affect individual people or businesses—
but that's not the case. In fact, many people share the loss indirectly. In
the example of the girl stealing CDs from a store, this may cause the store
to lose money, which forces it to raise prices to continue operating. Thus,
everyone who buys music at that store pays for the stolen CDs indirectly.
In the example of the accountant taking money from his company, the
same sort of thing might happen. If the company loses too much money,
then it might have to cut jobs in order to make a profit, or it might need to
raise the prices of its goods or services. At any rate, other people will feel
the impact of the company's loss. Many people are impacted—without
ever realizing it—by the financial losses due to theft and embezzlement.

Thus, when we read that larceny-theft accounts for a total loss of
4.9 billion dollars per year and that embezzlement accounts for an es-
timated loss of 50 billion dollars per year, we can begin to understand
how this affects everyone. People pay more for their own car insurance
because other people's cars get stolen, or they pay more for health care
because of fraudulent health-care payments or dishonest accountants.
One way that everyone pays for financial losses due to crime is through
taxes. Taxes pay for the judicial courts that hear the trials of thieves and
embezzlers, the police who investigate crime, and for the prisons that
punish the guilty.

Beyond that social injustice, lies an even deeper inequity in the justice system. According to the *Sourcebook of Criminal Justice*, published

LARCENY AND EMBEZZLEMENT

Both larceny and embezzlement are ways to steal money. They are different in the way that the thief takes the money. In larceny, the thief usually physically takes the money or the goods that are stolen. Larceny involves changing the ownership of the thing that is stolen. Taking money from a person's wallet when they aren't looking is larceny. In embezzlement, the thief uses the trust a company or organization has in him to take money the company has given him for some other purpose. For example, a store manager might say he bought new furniture for his office, and shows the storeowner a false receipt for the furniture. The storeowner then might give the manager money for the furniture, even though he didn't actually spend that much for the furniture. Thus, the manager steals money from the company.

by the Bureau of Crime Statistics, the average prison sentence for someone convicted of embezzlement is just 16.5 months. The average sentence for someone convicted of larceny, on the other hand, is 28.3 months—nearly a full year longer than a convicted embezzler despite the average loss due to larceny being much lower. In other words, people who commit white-collar crimes are not punished as severely as people who commit blue-collar crimes.

For example, the Lynchburg, Virginia, *News and Advance* reported on January 5, 2005, that a man had stolen over 300,000 dollars from a company where he worked as a midlevel manager. He had done this by submitting false expense reports and pocketing the extra money. He was found guilty of embezzlement by the court and sentenced to only one year in prison.

If the person stealing this car is caught, he will face a longer sentence than if he had embezzled hundreds of thousands of dollars.

Think about that for a moment. Stealing 300,000 dollars is the equivalent of stealing fifteen 20,000-dollar cars. Yet, anybody convicted of stealing that many cars would almost certainly be imprisoned for longer than one year. In fact, according to the *Sourcebook of Criminal Justice Statistics,* the average prison sentence for people convicted of motor vehicle theft is almost 130 months. If the man reported in the Lynchburg *News and Advance* were sentenced by these same guidelines, he would be in prison for 1,950 months, or 162.5 years.

Why is there such a huge difference in sentencing standards for these crimes? Some people believe that white-collar criminal offenders are less likely to repeat their crimes because their wealth allows them to live comfortably without resorting to crime. Supporters of this theory point out that white-collar criminal offenders, because of their education and technical skills, can serve the public interest better outside prison, and therefore require shorter prison sentences.

Other people disagree, saying that the different standards of sentencing punish the economically disadvantaged unfairly. These people might point out that the sentencing guidelines are written by educated people who work white-collar jobs, and that poor, uneducated people are left out of the lawmaking process. They might also say that the differences in sentencing standards reflect the fear that wealthy people feel toward poor people.

The truth probably lies somewhere between these two positions. Socioeconomic discrimination can be a difficult thing to identify in courts and prisons. Often, as in the case of public defenders, the problems don't lie in the procedures of the justice system as much as they do in the way those procedures are implemented from one place to another. One public defender, for example, might be excellent and be very concerned for the welfare of her clients. Another, however, might be too lazy to put much effort into proving his clients innocent.

Some of these differences may occur geographically. If standards of justice vary from one place to another, is that fair?

CHAPTER 4

AN UNFAIR SYSTEM?

"Our system is not one of justice, but of law."
—Edna Buchanan, crime reporter and novelist

Possession and use of narcotic drugs is a crime in North America. Whether a person is arrested for drug possession in San Francisco or Saskatoon, if she is found guilty she will face punishment. That is true no matter where she is.

However, the degree of punishment a person will receive varies greatly, depending on where he is arrested and what court hears the case. In Delaware, for instance, it is common for people possessing small amounts of marijuana to be placed on probation for a few years by the courts. In Nevada, possession of twenty-eight grams (one ounce) or less marijuana could result in a fine of six hundred dollars, but no time in prison. Canadian law dictates a fine of 150 dollars for possession of fifteen grams or less, while larger amounts could result in prison time.

Some of the most striking differences occur between the federal and state courts in the United States. Two separate cases—both in Iowa— help illustrate this difference.

FEDERAL VS. STATE COURTS

In the first case, an Iowa man was arrested while in possession of 190 grams of methamphetamines—an amount so large that it was obvious he intended to sell it. It was the man's first drug offense, though. The judge in the Iowa state court sentenced the man to two years of probation, one hundred hours of community service, and a fine of one thousand dollars. Since the man was a police officer, he was dismissed from his job.

In the second case, an Iowa woman was arrested while in possession of 188 grams of methamphetamines, just two grams less than the man in the first example. Like the man, she was also a first-time drug offender. The similarities end there, however. The woman's case was not heard in an Iowa state court, but rather in U.S. federal court. A federal judge sentenced her to thirteen years in prison without the possibility of parole.

The reason behind the stiff punishment in the second example is mandatory sentencing guidelines at the federal level. These guidelines, established in 1987, specified the punishments that could be used in criminal cases. They were developed to improve consistency between federal sentences from one place to another. Thus, regardless of which federal court tried a person, whether in Montana or Hawaii, the sentence would be the same. While the intent of mandatory sentencing guidelines was admira-

Sentences for the same crime vary across the United States.

ble, many people disagreed with the sentences set forth in those guidelines.

Penalties for drug offenders in particular were very harsh. At the time, President Ronald Reagan was pursuing the "War on Drugs," and politicians were eager to wage the war with tough *rhetoric* and even tougher judicial action. Whether the severe punishments established in 1987 helped to decrease drug use in the United States is a question still debated today. However, it is indisputable that judges had little leeway to change a sentence, and many people were sentenced to long prison terms because of the mandatory sentencing guidelines. This helped cause an explosion in the U.S. prison population, which is now the largest prison system in the world.

Today, the U.S. prison system incarcerates more than two million people. Given the total population of the United States, that means that approximately 1 out of every 145 people in the country are in some form of judicial incarceration. In 2001, 56 percent of the federal prison population was imprisoned on drug charges. The huge inmate population has

The consequences for the possession of powder cocaine are not as serious as for crack.

strained prisons throughout the country and has led to many other problems within the prison system. (We look at these in greater depth in chapter 6.)

While many people believe mandatory sentencing guidelines helped foster greater equity in federal courts, others maintain that the guidelines for drug convictions actually discriminate against minorities. Critics point to the differences between sentence guidelines for possession of crack cocaine and powder cocaine as a reason for this.

CRACK VS. POWDER COCAINE

Under the mandatory sentencing guidelines, possession of five grams of crack cocaine mandates a minimum sentence of five years in prison. For powder cocaine, on the other hand, it takes five hundred grams of the drug to mandate the same prison term. According to the guidelines then, crack cocaine is one hundred times worse than powder cocaine in a criminal court. That alone would not elicit any major criticism but for two reasons.

First, minorities are statistically more likely to use crack cocaine than are whites. This could be due to economic disparities between the races. Crack cocaine is much less expensive than powder cocaine, and therefore more easily available. As a result, more than 90 percent of all convictions for possession of crack cocaine involve minorities—particularly African Americans.

The second reason to believe the mandatory sentencing guidelines discriminate against minorities is the fact that whites are more likely to be tried before a state court than a federal one. The mandatory sentencing guidelines only apply to federal courts. Thus, a trial in a state court—as in the two examples from Iowa earlier in this chapter—is likely to result in a more lenient sentence.

Supporters of the mandatory sentencing guidelines point out that users of crack cocaine are more likely to threaten the peace and safety of a community. Thus, they claim, mandatory sentencing guidelines actu-

In 2005, the Supreme Court ruled that mandatory sentences were not constitutional.

ally reflect the desires of communities around the country to keep their neighborhoods safe.

Whether racially motivated or not, the U.S. Supreme Court overturned the federal mandatory sentencing guidelines on January 12, 2005. Although the guidelines are no longer mandatory, they will still serve as recommendations to shape judges' sentencing decisions. The ruling may help alleviate some of the pressures on the overburdened prison system. However, without the consistency that mandated sentences provided, the change may also lead to greater sentencing disparities, possibly causing inequities in the way criminal offenders are punished at the federal level.

CRIMINAL VS. CIVIL TRIALS

Beyond the differences between different court jurisdictions—state or federal, for example—are other ways court procedures create apparent disparities in sentences and verdicts. One of the most highly publicized court cases in North American legal history illustrates one such disparity.

On June 12, 1994, Nicole Brown Simpson and Ronald Goldman were found murdered outside Brown's home in Los Angeles, California. The grisly details of the murder were enough to draw instant and glaring media attention to the case. Making the case even more intriguing was the fact that Nicole Brown Simpson had been married to a popular and successful celebrity—O. J. Simpson, a professional football Hall of Famer and actor.

Over the course of the next sixteen months, television cameras and talk show personalities followed the legal proceedings as Simpson became a defendant in a murder trial. The trial itself was a showcase for many of the inequities discussed in this book. For example, Mark Furhman—a detective who had found a key piece of evidence for the prosecution—was accused by the defense of being a racist. The defense team claimed that Furhman had planted the evidence at Simpson's house in order to frame him for the murder.

Although the jury found Simpson not guilty of the murders, he would again find himself in court in 1997 because of the incident. This time, however, the trial took place in a civil court rather than a criminal court. Despite the not guilty verdict in the criminal trial, Simpson was found legally liable in the civil trial for the deaths of Nicole Brown Simpson and Ronald Goldman. As a result, Simpson was required to pay over thirty-three million dollars in damages.

Many people who had followed the criminal trial on television were perplexed. How could O. J. Simpson be found innocent of murder in one trial and then be found liable, or responsible, for it in another? The reason lies in the distinction between the two types of courts that heard the trials.

Criminal courts conduct trials of people who are suspected of violating the law. Those who are found guilty of breaking the law are punished, while those who are found innocent are allowed to go free. Civil trials, on the other hand, do not necessarily involve a violation of the law. In a civil trial, a plaintiff seeks to claim compensation from a defendant for some damage or harm done. In the case of the O. J. Simpson civil trial, Ronald Goldman's family sought to get monetary compensation from Simpson, whom they believed had killed their son and brother.

An even more important distinction in this case is the difference in how juries reach their decisions in criminal and civil trials. In a criminal trial, the jury is instructed to convict the defendant only if the prosecution can prove "beyond any reasonable doubt" that the defendant is guilty. In other words, if a juror has any reasonable doubts that perhaps the defendant did not do what she stands accused of, then the juror is required to return a verdict of not guilty. In the Simpson criminal trial, the jury had reasonable doubts that he had committed the murders. Thus, he was found not guilty.

In a civil trial, on the other hand, the jury is instructed to find a defendant liable if the "*preponderance* of evidence" indicates he committed the crime of which he is accused. Even if the jury still has doubts, if the prosecution presents a stronger case against the defendant than the defense does in support of the defendant, then the jury must find the defendant liable for the damages claimed. In the Simpson civil trial, with-

WOULD O. J. BE IN PRISON IF HE WERE POOR?

The O. J. Simpson murder trial also illustrates the socioeconomic inequities between wealthy and poor criminal defendants. As a successful football player and actor, Simpson was able to afford a "Dream Team"—a team of expensive, high-profile lawyers whose skill had made them very successful in the courtroom. According to a 1995 Gallup-CNN/USA Today poll of 693 people, 73 percent of people believed that Simpson would have been convicted of murder if he were not wealthy. Even more—84 percent—believed that Simpson's team of lawyers had done a good job in the trial, thus securing a "not guilty" verdict.

out the benefit of reasonable doubt, he was found liable for the deaths of Nicole Brown Simpson and Ronald Goldman, and was thus ordered to pay compensation.

JURY BIAS

Simpson's two trials show us yet another facet of the justice system that we have already discussed in this book—racial bias. Aside from the claims that Mark Furhman was a racist, the verdicts of both trials *polarized* public attitudes in ways that less public trials could not. In a follow-up 1995 Gallup poll, only 36 percent of whites felt that the not guilty verdict in the criminal trial was correct. In contrast, 73 percent of African Americans thought it was correct. In a 1997 Gallup poll, the numbers were reversed. Fully 74 percent of whites believed the liable verdict in the civil trial was

O. J. Simpson's mug shot after his arrest

In O. J. Simpson's criminal trial, the jury was made up of ten women and two men. Of those twelve people, eight were African American, two were Hispanic, one was Native American, and one was white. Given the results of the Gallup polls, did the racial mix of the jury influence their decision to acquit Simpson?

correct, while only 26 percent of African Americans thought it was correct.

These numbers show us that racial bias is a very potent and persuasive force in courts of law. In fact, any sort of bias—whether based on gender, age, race, or anything else—can influence a jury's verdict. Although many people claim they would not be swayed by the race of the defendant or the plaintiff, it is clear from the two polls that Simpson's race played a part in many people's opinions. That brings us to the question of how an impartial and objective jury can possibly be selected when so many potential jurors have biases, whether they realize it or not.

When a case is brought to a jury trial, a pool of prospective jurors is selected randomly from the court's jurisdiction—the area that it serves—to hear the facts of the case and determine guilt or innocence in a criminal trial, or liability in a civil trial. Once the pool of jurors is selected, the judge who will be hearing the case and the lawyers who will be arguing it ask the prospective jurors questions to determine who among them will be fit to serve on the jury. Some of them may be automatically dismissed

Racial bias can shape a jury's decision.

if they appear to have an obvious or strong bias in the case, or if they personally know the people involved. If a lawyer or judge dismisses a prospective juror for a good reason, that juror is said to be dismissed "for cause." The purpose of for cause challenges is to maintain an **objective** and neutral jury to decide the case.

In addition, the defense and prosecution have the opportunity to dismiss a limited number of other jurors without giving a reason. Dismissing a juror in this way is called a **peremptory** challenge. Lawyers use these challenges to try to eliminate jurors they feel will be unfavorable to the outcome they want in the trial. Peremptory challenges work a bit like a draft in professional sports, but backward. Whereas in professional sports, teams select the players to be on their teams, in court, lawyers eliminate jurors they don't want on their "team."

For example, a prosecuting attorney might dismiss housewives because she thinks they will be more lenient than women employed outside the home. A defense attorney, on the other hand, might dismiss people with college educations because he feels educated people might not

Lawyers can dismiss a limited number of prospective jurors without giving a reason.

be swayed by emotional appeals. In either case, it is the lawyer's discretion alone that determines whether a potential juror will be dismissed. In most cases, the lawyers do not need to justify their decisions regarding peremptory challenges.

While the effect of for cause challenges is clearly to make a more objective and impartial jury, the effect of peremptory challenges appears

A lawyer's use of peremptory challenges can lead to a biased jury.

to be quite the opposite. Rather than eliminating potential jurors whose personal beliefs and attitudes could influence their decisions on a case, peremptory challenges actually allow lawyers to try to shape the jury based on those attitudes—or at least based on what they perceive those attitudes to be. Of course, both the defense and the prosecution have the opportunity to eliminate jurors through peremptory challenges. Ideally, then, this evens the playing field, so to speak, and provides the court with a jury whose biases cancel each other out.

Unfortunately, in some instances the use of peremptory challenges leads to biased juries. However, the U.S. Supreme Court has continued to refine the process of jury selection by ruling that it is unconstitutional to exclude potential jurors based on arbitrary identifying characteristics such as age, gender, or race.

Looking back at the different verdicts in the two Simpson cases, as well as the examples of drug possession sentences in Iowa, we can see that differing opinions on issues in criminal justice cover a wide range. Whether you believe one sentence is more appropriate than another depends largely on how you understand the facts of the case and on your own personal viewpoint. Such is the nature of justice in a democracy. It is the will of the people that becomes the law of the land. People, as we all know, don't always agree on everything, and nothing is absolute.

There is no perfect justice system. Mistakes happen, and sometimes an innocent person goes to prison or a guilty person goes free. More frequently, as in our examples from Iowa, a person gets what might seem like too harsh of a punishment, or too lenient. If there were a perfectly correct way to determine all of these things, then we wouldn't need a judicial system.

CHAPTER 5

POLITICAL INEQUITIES

Give me your tired, your poor,
Your huddled masses yearning to breathe free,
The wretched refuse of your teeming shore.
Send these, the homeless, tempest-tost to me,
I lift my lamp beside the golden door!
—Emma Lazarus, "The New Colossus"

The populations of both Canada and the United States are made up of immigrants. Native Americans and First Nations (the Canadian term for American Indians) constitute only a very small percentage of the population of North America. Everybody else can trace their heritage back to some other part of the world—Europe, Asia, Africa, South or Central America, or Oceania.

Given the "melting pot" nature of North America, one would think that North Americans would welcome foreigners and accept new cultures. Sadly, this has not always been the case. Particularly in times of war or conflict, the people and governments of Canada and the United States have chosen to safeguard national security over the rights of individuals.

NORTH AMERICAN CONCENTRATION CAMPS

On December 7, 1941, Japanese fighter-planes and miniature submarines attacked the American naval fleet stationed at Pearl Harbor, Hawaii. The

The battle at Pearl Harbor on December 7, 1941

attack decimated the American fleet and killed over two thousand American servicemen and civilians. The next day, President Franklin D. Roosevelt declared war against Japan, entering the United States into World War II.

In both the United States and Canada, the attack on Pearl Harbor caused a ripple of fear, paranoia, and activity. All along the Pacific Coast of both countries, frightened citizens began to suspect their Japanese American neighbors of spying for the Japanese government or of being enemy combatants in waiting. On February 19, 1942, just two months after the attack, President Roosevelt signed into law Executive Order 9066, which allowed the military to declare large areas of land as forbidden to any or all people. A similar law in Canada—the War Measures Act—had been adopted in 1914 during World War I and was again invoked after the attack on Pearl Harbor.

Both Executive Order 9066 in the United States and the War Measures Act in Canada allowed the government to declare large areas, including the entire Pacific coastline, off-limits to people of Japanese ancestry. This forced many Japanese Americans to move away from their homes. Soon, both the Canadian and U.S. governments had established "relocation camps." These camps were essentially prisons where people of Japanese ancestry were required to live during World War II.

In the United States, about 120,000 Japanese American people—most of them American citizens born in the country—were sent to the camps. Almost 21,000 Japanese Canadians were sent to camps; fully 75 percent were Canadian citizens. In both cases, the camps were little more than desolate prisons in inhospitable areas of the North American West. Armed guards and barbed-wire fences kept the inhabitants of the camps from leaving, while strict curfew rules and austere living conditions made life difficult and joyless. Late in the war, President Roosevelt would refer to the relocation camps as "concentration camps," drawing a parallel between them and the infamous death camps of Nazi Germany.

Many of the people incarcerated in the relocation camps were forced to live there for as long as four years while the war continued in the Pacific against Japan. During that time, a long list of innocent people died in the prisons. Some died from poor medical care exacerbated by the stressful

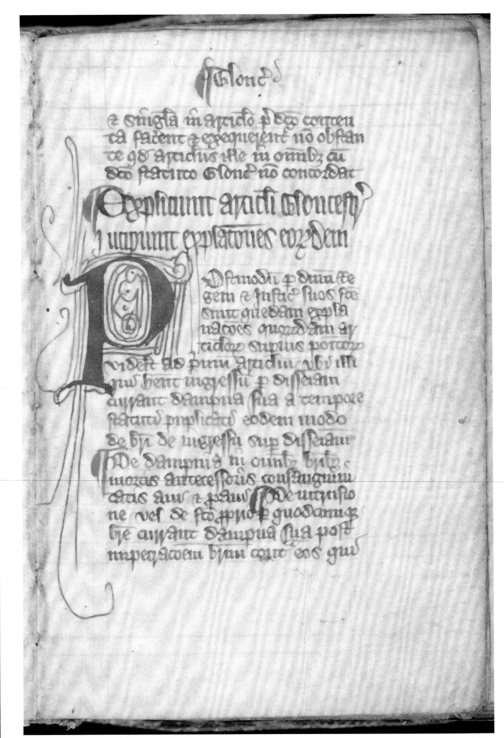

The Magna Carta, written in 1215, is the foundation for much of our legal system today.

THE 442ND REGIMENTAL COMBAT TEAM

Despite all of the distrust and fear Japanese Americans faced in their own country during World War II, a Japanese American combat battalion—the 442nd Regimental Combat Team—served with distinction in the European theater of World War II. In one battle, they suffered over eight hundred casualties in order to rescue another trapped American battalion. In 1946, President Truman greeted members of the 442nd at the White House, thanking them for their service and saying, "[You] fought not only the enemy but you fought prejudice— and you have won."

living condition imposed on them. Several other people were shot dead by guards, many of them under questionable circumstances.

Despite this, the people of Japanese ancestry who were forced to live in these camps were never given any benefit of due process of law in either Canada or the United States. Due process of law is a concept that guarantees protection of people's legal rights. It lies at the very heart of North American judicial ideology.

Although it was not called due process of law at the time, the concept was first set forth in 1215 in the Magna Carta, an agreement between King John of England and his barons. The Magna Carta restricted the powers of the king and stated that even the king had to follow the law. One of the most important clauses contained in the Magna Carta for the development of due process of law was Article 39, which stated: "No free man shall be arrested, or imprisoned, or deprived of his property, or outlawed, or exiled, or in any way destroyed, nor shall we (the king) go against him

A Japanese internment camp in California in 1942

or send against him, unless by legal judgment of his peers, or by the law of the land."

Article 39 established a check on the power of the king, opening the way for later ***constitutional democracies*** such as Canada and the United States. The Fifth Amendment to the United States Constitution uses very similar language to guarantee protection to people's personal rights: "No person shall be . . . deprived of life, liberty, or property, without due process of law; nor shall private property be taken for public use, without just compensation." In other words, the government cannot ***arbitrarily*** act against citizens without taking them to a fair and unbiased court.

Clearly, in the case of the Japanese internment camps of World War II, the rights of both Canadian and American citizens were denied, and due process was not followed. Even more outrageous was the fact that in 1944, the Nisei—second-generation Japanese American citizens—became eligible for the military draft. Even though their own rights were being severely restricted by the government and they were relocated due to doubts about their loyalty to the country, they could be forced to serve in the U.S. military. Many Japanese Americans resisted the draft and were sentenced to prison for their refusal.

After World War II, the internment camps closed and the Japanese Americans and Japanese Canadians were allowed to return to their homes. Not until 1988 did the people who had been confined to the camps finally receive some compensation for their ordeals. In that year, the governments of Canada and the United States both agreed to pay the survivors and victims of the internment camps a small settlement—twenty thousand dollars in the United States and twenty-one thousand dollars in Canada.

Many historians and social scientists agree that the Japanese internment camps of World War II were a reaction to the ***paranoia*** and fear that many people felt during the war. Some even believe that President Roosevelt secretly disapproved of the camps, agreeing to them only because he felt that Japanese Americans would be targeted by violence in their homes if they were not relocated to safety. The important question then, is not whether the relocation camps violated the rights of people

A converted horse stall was used to house Japanese detainees during World War II.

THE GENEVA CONVENTIONS

The Geneva Conventions are a set of treaties that set forth rules governing how war can be fought and how civilians, prisoners, and enemy combatants must be treated. They were developed to help avoid some of the atrocities that sometimes were committed in wars.

of Japanese ancestry to due process of law; rather, the question to ask is whether that violation of personal rights was justified.

SUSPECTED TERRORISTS AND DUE PROCESS

The same question could be asked today under slightly different circumstances. Today, the U.S. Navy operates a military base in Guantanamo Bay, Cuba. The land on which the base stands is leased by the United States from the government of Cuba according to an agreement reached between the two countries in 1903. In 2002, the United States began to hold prisoners of the war on terrorism in the Guantanamo Bay naval base. Several hundred prisoners from Afghanistan and elsewhere who were suspected of being linked to al-Qaeda, the Taliban, or any terrorist organization were detained in Guantanamo Bay without the benefit of due process of law.

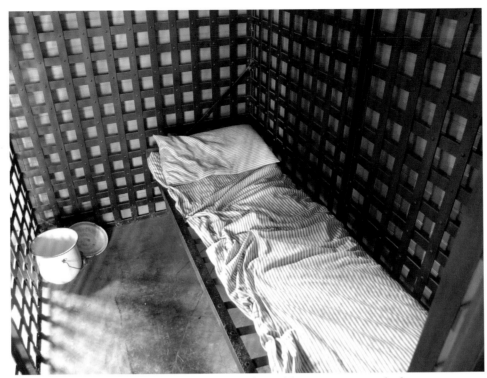

Do all prisoners deserve due process—or is the public interest served when some individuals are imprisoned without respect for their rights?

The United States classified these prisoners as "illegal enemy combatants." Under the international Geneva Conventions, this classification allows the military greater flexibility in dealing with the prisoners, as they are accorded fewer rights than they would be if they were deemed "legal enemy combatants." However, in order for any country to classify prisoners as illegal enemy combatants, that country must first hold tribunals—trials—to prove that they are. The United States, as of 2005, has refused to hold trials according to the Geneva Conventions.

Beyond the detention of suspected terrorists and enemy combatants, numerous reports written by former prisoners released in 2004 claim that American military personnel torture and abuse the prisoners at Guantanamo Bay, and that conditions in the prison are generally deplorable. American officials have denied these reports, saying that the prison is run under very high standards.

The U.S. administration and military maintain that the detention of suspected terrorists and enemy combatants is necessary for pursuing the war on terrorism. They say that information given to them by prisoners at Guantanamo Bay has helped them to find terrorist leaders and to stamp out terrorism throughout the world. For the U.S. government, the war on terror justifies the incarceration of hundreds of possible enemy combatants.

Opponents and critics, however, claim the prison violates the right of individuals to be presumed innocent until proven guilty in a court of law, one of the central ideas behind due process of law. Some of the prisoners in Guantanamo, they say, have been held prisoner for several years now without ever receiving a trial to determine their innocence or guilt. Other people say the prison is actually doing more harm than good in the war on terrorism because of the negative impact it has on public and foreign relations.

What is certain is that the prisoners are being held without the benefit of due process of law. Whether the circumstances in this situation justify that is still debatable and likely will continue to be for a very long time. The issue points to an interesting question: Does due process of law always serve the public interest? Just as with many of the issues brought up in this book, people have many different opinions on the matter but no solid answers.

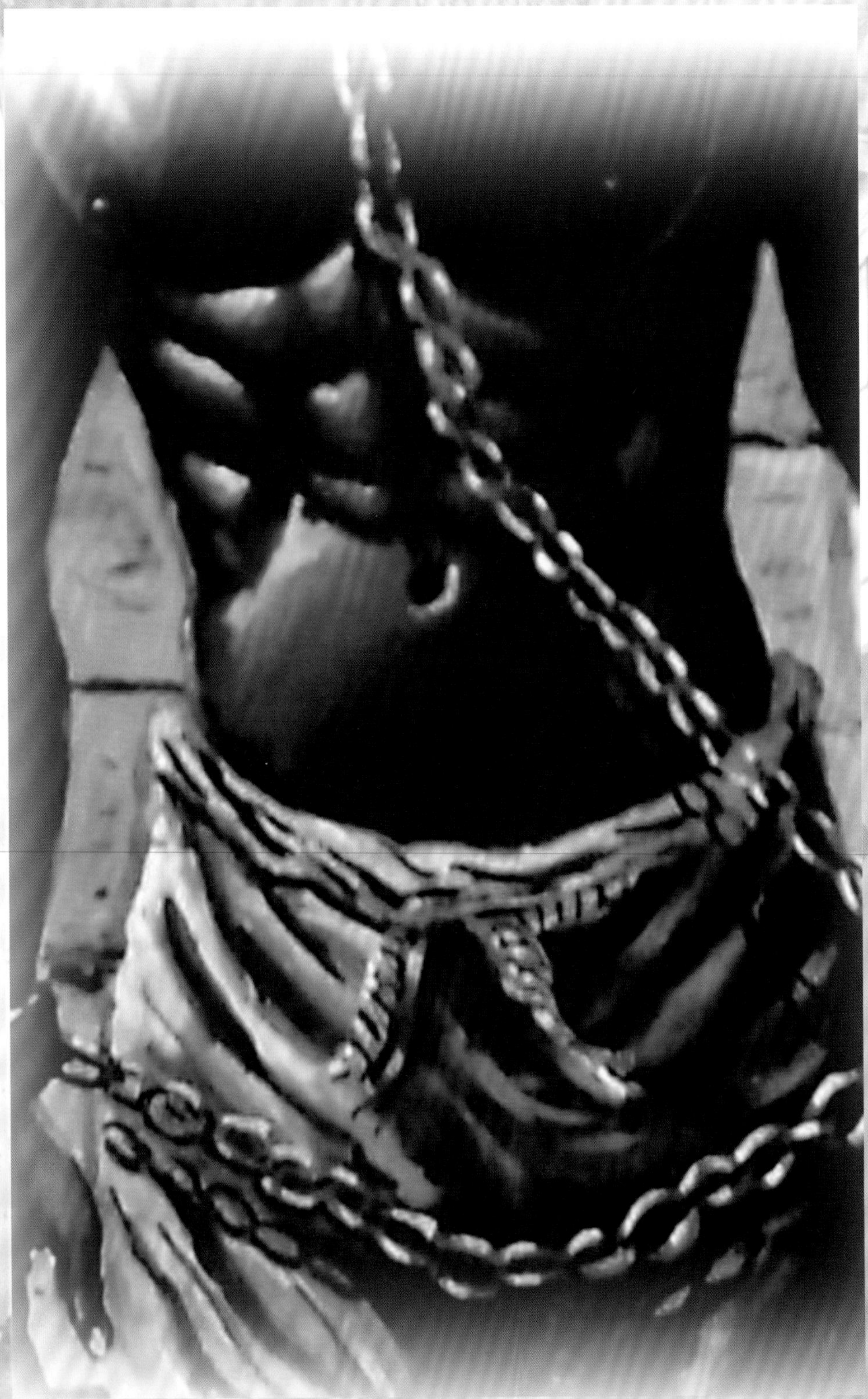

CHAPTER 6

THE INJUSTICE OF PRISON LIFE

I am the way into the doleful city,
I am the way to eternal grief,
I am the way to a forsaken race.
Justice it was that moved my great creator . . .
Abandon every hope, all you who enter.
—Dante Alighieri, Inferno, canto III

In 2004, people watched in disgust as stories of prisoner abuse and degradation unfolded on television screens around the world. The infamous Abu Ghraib prison in Iraq had once been the site of torture and executions under the regime of former Iraqi dictator Saddam Hussein. As many as four thousand political prisoners were believed to have been executed there in 1984 alone.

Inside the "death chamber" at Abu Ghraib

UNCOOPERATIVE CORRECTIONS OFFICERS

At one point during the Stanford Prison Experiment, one of the "guards" thought the basement of the Psychology Department wasn't secure enough. He asked the local police department if they could move the "prisoners" to an unused block of cells at the local jail. The police said they couldn't allow people to stay in the jail, for insurance reasons. Later, the experiment guard recalled that he became very angry and frustrated at the lack of cooperation between the two correctional facilities.

In 2003, Saddam Hussein's regime fell, brought down by the might of British and American military forces, along with several of their allies. People throughout the world thought the tragic abuses that had marked the Hussein regime would end. Surely such abuses couldn't possibly occur under the supervision of a democratic country like the United States? And yet, Abu Ghraib once again became a focal point for media and public attention.

This time, American military personnel were caught on film subjecting Iraqi prisoners of war to violence, threats of injury, and sexual abuses. The pictures were graphic and disturbing, and prompted outrage throughout the world. Investigations would find a long list of misdeeds by a small number of American military prison personnel. Investigators also discovered that one of the Iraqi inmates, Manadel al-Jamadi, had died as a result of torturous interrogation techniques used by prison staff.

The whole incident stained American prestige abroad and caused many Americans to question their leadership and the way in which the

war on terrorism was being waged. For those familiar with psychological research and prison psychology, however, the Abu Ghraib abuse scandal was perhaps not such a big surprise.

PRISON PSYCHOLOGY

In 1971, Stanford University psychology professor Philip Zimbardo conducted a famous experiment into the social and psychological effects of prison. In the experiment, twelve young men were chosen at random to act as prison guards, and twelve other young men were chosen at random to act as prisoners. The twenty-four men were chosen from an original pool of seventy individuals, and were picked because Zimbardo and his team of researchers believed they were the most psychologically stable and healthy men in the original pool.

The "prisoners" were given no instructions on what was expected of them. Their role would simply be to act as they would if they were in prison. The "guards" were likewise given few instructions. They were told that it was their duty to run the prison, with only one requirement—physical violence was not permitted.

Almost immediately, the experiment took on a frightening life of its own. By the second day of the experiment, the guards had become abusive and domineering, forcing the prisoners to do embarrassing acts and physically demanding exercises. The guards also punished the prisoners in a variety of ways, including placing them in solitary confinement and refusing to give them food. Afterward, many of the guards expressed disappointment that the experiment was ending—they had apparently enjoyed being guards in their mock prison.

The prisoners also underwent a powerful transformation due to the psychological stress and humiliation they were forced to endure during the experiment. Some reacted to the experiment by actively resisting the will of the guards. Others became model prisoners, doing everything they could to please the guards. Still others simply broke down mentally and emotionally, crying and becoming confused. Several of the

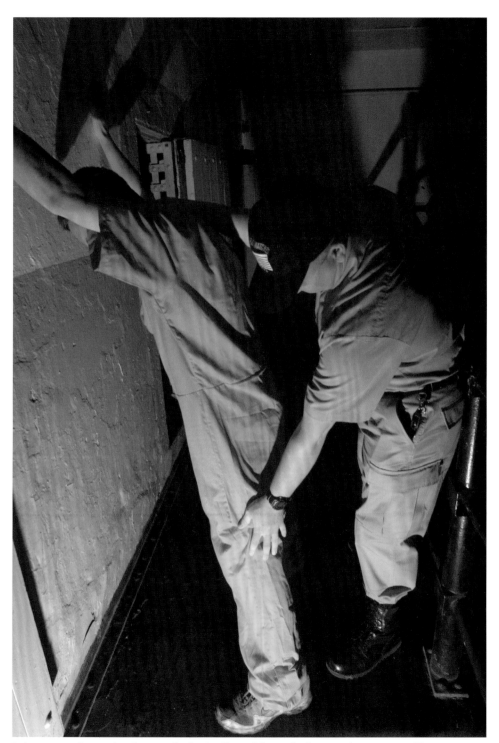

Prison guards need to be psychologically stable and adequately supported by administration to resist the pressures of prison life.

The experience of being a prisoner can change individuals psychologically.

The interactions between prisoner and guard can be fraught with power issues.

prisoners showed extreme psychological distress. One even developed a rash on his entire body as a result of stress.

The results of the Stanford Prison Experiment were so disturbing that Professor Zimbardo canceled it after only six days, although it had been scheduled to run for two full weeks. The experiment showed that ordinary people—psychologically stable and healthy individuals—can easily become abusive when placed in positions of power over other people, particularly when there is little supervision from higher authorities.

The experiment has been used to help explain how such atrocities as the German death camps of World War II could have been committed. More recently, of course, the Abu Ghraib prisoner abuse scandal has been viewed through the lens of the Stanford Prison Experiment.

The experiment also forces us to question many of the practices that are maintained in our prison systems today. Do abuses such as those

Women in prison are especially vulnerable to abuse from guards.

recorded in the Stanford Prison Experiment happen in American and Canadian prisons, or are those sorts of behaviors only seen in remote places like the Abu Ghraib prison?

Sadly, reports abound of abuses committed against prisoners at all levels of incarceration. While there are numerous instances of male inmates reporting mistreatment at the hands of guards and prison staff, perhaps the most serious and most disturbing reports are those that involve female inmates.

WOMEN IN PRISON

A female inmate in a Washington state correctional facility reported that one of the male guards in the correctional facility had raped her, and that she had born a child as a result of the rape. The guard denied having had any sexual contact with the inmate. Later, paternity tests showed that the man was indeed the father of the child. Despite this, no criminal charges were ever filed against the guard. Indeed, he even tried to gain custody of the child, though his bid was unsuccessful.

Or take the example of the male prison guard who was accused of raping or sexually assaulting three different female inmates. None of the women came forward to tell their stories or report the male guard's misconduct. Instead, the state Department of Corrections received an anonymous tip that the guard was using his position of power in the prison to exploit some of the female inmates. It was not until investigators came to the correctional facility and began to ask questions of other female inmates that the extent of the man's abuses became clear. Even once the government officials began to ask their questions, the women were reluctant to answer honestly, fearing that the guard might try to enact some sort of reprisal, or revenge, on them. When the full scale of the man's abuses became clear, he was immediately fired from his job. No criminal charges were filed in the case, however.

These sorts of weak reactions to cases of abuse of female inmates by male prison staff do little to deter future incidents. Not only do they not help prevent such incidents from occurring, but they also discourage female inmates from reporting any such abuses. According to Amnesty International USA, several states have no laws at all regarding cross-gender supervision in prisons. Several other states also have laws in place that actually make it possible to penalize inmates who have sexual relations with guards. At first glance that might seem to make some sense. However, as we saw in the last example, a guard has a great deal of power over the inmates in a prison and can use that power to **coerce** female inmates into a relationship for fear of being punished.

Recent trends in crime rates are bringing these issues into the public eye with a great deal of urgency. According to the FBI Uniform Crime Report, in the ten-year period from 1993 to 2002, the number of arrests of male offenders dropped by 5.9 percent. In that same period, arrests of female offenders rose by 14.1 percent. Over that same period, according to the Bureau of Justice Statistics Bulletin, the number of female prison inmates in the United States rose from 55,365 in 1993 to 97,491 in 2002, an increase of 76 percent over ten years.

Many former inmates face more injustice on the other side of the prison fence.

With the number of female inmates in prison continuing to rise rapidly, cross-gender supervision and abuse issues will also likely continue to become more prominent. Although many people today are concerned with the abuse itself, many others are beginning to address the impact that such abuses—and indeed, prison in general—have on both men and women.

AFTER PRISON:
MORE INJUSTICE

In 2002, Scott Hornoff, a former police detective, took his first steps beyond the walls of the prison where he had been incarcerated since 1995 for a murder he did not commit. From prison, he had struggled to clear his name and overturn his conviction until 2002, when the real murderer confessed to the crime, and Hornoff was released. Once outside of prison, however, he found that he had to struggle to live a normal life.

In an ABC News interview on December 9, 2004, Hornoff described the sorts of adjustments that he had to make after being released from prison. Despite having been a police officer himself, he found that police officers and security guards made him uneasy. He also said that it took a long while before he felt comfortable doing things without needing to ask permission first. What's more, he discovered that wherever he went, people labeled him as a criminal or a convict, even though his conviction was overturned and he was declared innocent.

Scott Hornoff's story would be familiar to many people released from prison, whether they had been sentenced correctly or not. What then of all the people, many of them whose stories have never been told, who have suffered humiliation and abuse at the hands of unscrupulous prison personnel, or even at the hands of fellow inmates? How much more difficult are the adjustments that they must make in order to regain a semblance of normalcy in their lives?

Fortunately, progress has been steadily made on improving the justice and prison systems of North America. Much of this progress has

The scales of justice are not always equally weighted.

No matter what their crime, prisoners deserve justice. But how do we define justice?

been championed by organizations and individuals who have made it their cause to try to promote justice in the justice system, which—as we have seen—is not perfect.

CHAPTER 7

Evolving Justice

> *"They always say time changes things, but you actually have to change them yourself."*
> —Andy Warhol, *The Philosophy of Andy Warhol*

We have already seen that the United States has the largest prison population in the world. But as with many of the statistics we have looked at, that fact does not tell the whole story.

One reason for the large prison population in the United States is strict enforcement of drug laws, particularly at the federal level. However, with the Supreme Court ruling that sentencing guidelines are no longer mandatory, many people who were sentenced under those guidelines may be released from prison or their terms will be reduced. It is also possible that fewer arrests for drug possession will result in incarceration, which will help reduce the prison population in the future.

Another point to consider is that prisons in North America are far more humane than prisons in many other countries. Inmates in most prisons have access to education, counseling, television, books, and athletic equipment. By comparison, North American inmates are well fed and receive medical care.

Looking at prisons in many other countries, we see unhealthy and unsanitary conditions, with correspondingly high inmate death rates. In

The S21 Prison in Cambodia was the starting point for the notorious "killing fields." More than 11,000 prisoners were sent here, tortured, and murdered along with their families. Only twelve survived.

In most cases, North American prisons have better conditions than those in many parts of the world.

countries like Iraq under Saddam Hussein, people suspected of opposing the government were executed without a trial. Despite the inequities that we may see in the justice systems of North America, conditions in many countries are much worse.

Americans and Canadians strive for government excellence. Some aspects of our criminal justice systems can definitely be improved—but many people and a long list of organizations have worked to make a positive difference and promote social justice.

AMNESTY INTERNATIONAL

Perhaps the largest and best known of these organizations is Amnesty International, with a global membership of 1.8 million. Amnesty International campaigns for human rights throughout the world. According to their Web site, Amnesty International's goal "is to undertake research and action focused on preventing and ending grave abuses of the rights to physical and mental integrity, freedom of conscience and expression, and freedom from discrimination, within the context of its work to promote all human rights."

Many of the projects undertaken by Amnesty International involve attempting to influence lawmakers to reform laws the organization sees as harsh or unfair. In the United States, one of those projects is an attempt to reform certain laws regarding the relationships of prison staff with female inmates. Amnesty International would like to ban all sexual relationships between staff and inmates, and to make the staff accountable for any such violations. As discussed in the last chapter, laws of this sort would help protect the rights and safety of female inmates.

Amnesty International also seeks to promote the comfort and care of pregnant inmates. Currently, many states allow pregnant inmates to be shackled or restrained outside prison grounds, just as any other inmate would be. The organization believes that such treatment of pregnant women is degrading and unnecessary. One of Amnesty International's primary beliefs is that all people are deserving of respect, and that laws should preserve that respect.

Many North American individuals and organizations are working to ensure that the standards of true justice are met.

The Torch of Liberty is an ideal that should inspire us all.

OTHER ORGANIZATIONS AND INDIVIDUALS WORKING FOR JUSTICE

Another organization that works to promote justice in North America is the Innocence Project. Founded in 1992 at the Benjamin N. Cardozo School of Law, the Innocence Project works as a nonprofit legal clinic for economically disadvantaged people convicted of crimes. Specifically, the Innocence Project works with DNA testing to try to prove people innocent.

No less determined than organizations like the Innocence Project and Amnesty International, individual people have made significant contributions to prison and legal reforms in the hopes of making a more equitable and just judicial system. Many of them offer their time and effort in whatever way they can, large or small, to try to make a difference. Some are drawn to this sort of work simply because they believe in their cause. Others are drawn to it because they or someone they love has suffered some sort of injustice in the past.

Law in a democracy is constantly evolving. Although it is written in the halls of government, it is conceived and given shape in the hearts and minds of individual citizens. As a result, it is constantly being refined. Although total justice may still lie far away, the march toward that goal never ceases.

GLOSSARY

apathetic: Not taking an interest in anything.

arbitrarily: Based solely on personal wishes, feelings, or perceptions.

choreographed: Planned out.

coerce: Force someone to do something he or she does not want to do.

constitutional democracies: Governments in which the authority of the majority is limited by legal means such as a constitution.

court-martialed: Tried in a military court.

DNA samples: Samples of the nucleic acid molecule that is a major component of the chromosomes, carries genetic information, and can be used to establish identity when matched with evidence left at a crime scene.

draw: A tie.

fraud: The crime of obtaining money or other benefit by the use of deliberate deception.

gladiators: Professional fighters in ancient Rome who fought in an arena as public entertainment.

inherent: Innate or characteristic of something, and therefore unable to be considered separately.

lynching: The seizing of someone believed to have committed a crime and putting him or her to death immediately and without trial, often by hanging.

objective: Free of any bias or prejudice.

paranoia: Extreme and unreasonable suspicion of other people and their motives.

peremptory: Not open to debate or discussion.

polarized: Made differences between groups more clear-cut.

precedent: An action or decision that can be used as an example for a later decision or to justify a similar action.

preponderance: The majority.

prosecuting: Representing the state or the people in a criminal trial.

reformatory: A penal institution for young offenders.

rhetoric: Speech or writing that communicates its point persuasively.

skewed: Something made uneven, thereby misrepresenting the true meaning or nature of something.

slave economy: A financial system based on the use of slave labor.

FURTHER READING

Bogira, Steve. *Courtroom 302: A Year Behind the Scenes in an American Criminal Courthouse.* New York: Knopf Books for Young Readers, 2005.

Cadnum, Michael. *Rundown.* New York: Viking, 1999.

Cormier, Robert. *The Rag and Bone Shop.* New York: Delacorte Press, 2001.

Crowe, Chris. *Getting Away With Murder: The True Story of the Emmett Till Case.* New York: Dial Books, 2003.

Kowalski, Kathiann. *Teen Rights: At Home, at School, Online.* Berkeley Heights, N.J.: Enslow, 2000.

Kranz, Rachel. *Straight Talk About Prejudice.* New York: Facts On File, 2002.

Netzley, Patricia. *Issues in Crime.* San Diego, Calif.: Lucent Books, 2000.

Silverstein, Herma. *Threads of Evidence: Using Forensic Science to Solve Crimes.* New York: Twenty-First Century Books, 2005.

INEQUITIES OF THE JUSTICE SYSTEM

FOR MORE INFORMATION

Amnesty International
www.amnesty.org

David Milgaard—wrongful conviction in Canada
archives.cbc.ca/300c.asp?id=1-70-713

Duluth Lynchings
collections.mnhs.org/duluthlynchings

Innocence Project
www.innocenceproject.org

Children of the Camps: The Documentary
www.pbs.org/childofcamp

Michigan Supreme Court Learning Center
www.courts.michigan.gov/lc-gallery/lc-gallery1.htm

The Scottsboro Boys Case—discrimination in court
www.pbs.org/wgbh/amex/scottsboro

United States Courts
www.uscourts.gov

BIBLIOGRAPHY

Alexander, Meredith. "Thirty Years Later, Stanford Prison Experiment Lives On." *Stanford Report*, August 22, 2001. http://news-service.stanford.edu/news/2001/august22/prison2-a.html.

"An Unreasonable System." *Des Moines Register*, June 1, 1996. http://www.druglibrary.org/olsen/WAR/trimble6.html.

Anderson, John C. *Why Lawyers Derail Justice: Probing the Roots of Legal Injustices.* University Park: Pennsylvania State University Press, 1999.

Annual Estimates of the Population by Sex, Race and Hispanic or Latino Origin for the United States: April 1, 2000 to July 1, 2003. Washington, D.C.: United States Census Bureau, 2003.

Benson, Deborah. "A Stiffer Sentence than James Trimble's." *Des Moines Register*, July 4, 1996. http://www.pdxnorml.org/dare_trimble2.html.

Bloom, Barbara E., ed. *Gendered Injustice: Addressing Female Offenders.* Durham, N.C.: Carolina Academic Press, 2003.

Bright, Stephen B., and Patrick J. Keenan. "Judges and the Politics of Death: Deciding Between the Bill of Rights and the Next Election in Capital Cases." *Boston University Law Review* 73 (May 1995): 759.

Carollo, Kim. "Finding Solace After Wrongful Conviction." ABC News Internet Ventures, December 9, 2004. http://www.abcnews.go.com/us/story?id=315686&page=1.

"Children of the Camps." PBS Online, 1999. http://www.pbs.org/childofcamp.

Duluth Lynchings Online Resource. Minnesota Historical Society, 2003. http://collections.mnhs.org/duluthlynchings.

"The Duluth Tragedy." *Mankato Daily Free Press*, June 17, 1920. Courtesy of Minnesota Historical Society. http://collections.mnhs.org/duluthlynchings/details.cfm?DcmntID=90&Sequence=1&SentBy=Citations&bhcp=1.

Federal Bureau of Investigation. *Crime in the United States.* Washington, D.C.: Author, 2002.

Forst, Brian. *Errors of Justice: Nature, Sources and Remedies.* Cambridge: Cambridge University Press, 2004.

Gilliard, Darrell K., and Allen J. Beck. "Prisoners in 1993." *Bureau of Justice Statistics Bulletin.* Washington, D.C.: U.S. Department of Justice, June 1994.

Harrison, Paige M., and Allen J. Beck. "Prisoners in 2002." *Bureau of Justice Statistics Bulletin.* Washington, D.C.: U.S. Department of Justice, August 2003.

Hirsch, James S. *Hurricane: The Miraculous Journey of Rubin Carter.* New York: Houghton Mifflin, 2000.

Linder, Doug. "The Trial of Orenthal James Simpson." *Famous Trials*, 2000. http://www.law.umkc.edu/faculty/projects/ftrials/ftrials.htm.

Miller, Marilyn, and Marian Faux, eds. *The New York Public Library American History Desk Reference.* New York: Macmillan, 1997.

Reiman, Jeffrey. *The Rich Get Richer and the Poor Get Prison: Ideology, Class, and Criminal Justice*, 5th ed. Boston: Allyn and Bacon, 1998.

Rennison, Callie Marie, and Michael R. Rand. "Criminal Victimization." *National Crime Victimization Survey.* Washington, D.C.: U.S. Department of Justice, August 2003.

Savage, Charlie. "High Court Overturns Sentencing Guidelines." *Boston Globe*, January 13, 2005. http://www.boston.com/news/nation/washington/articles/2005/01/13/high_court_overturns_sentencing_guidelines.

United States Department of Justice. "Women in Prison." *Bureau of Justice Special Report.* Washington, D.C.: Author, 1991.

United States Department of Justice. "Criminal Victimization in the United States, 2002: Statistical Tables." *National Crime Victimization Survey*. Washington, D.C.: Author, December 2003.

United States Department of Justice. *Sourcebook of Criminal Justice Statistics Online.* Washington, D.C.: Bureau of Justice Statistics. 2003. http://www.albany.edu/sourcebook/pdf/t525.pdf.

Walker, Samuel, Cassia Spohn, and Miriam DeLone. *The Color of Justice: Race, Ethnicity and Crime in America*, 2nd ed. Stamford, Conn.: Wadsworth/Thomson Learning, 2000.

INDEX

PICTURE CREDITS

Chapter opening art was taken from a painting titled *Slave at Auction* by Raymond Gray.

Raymond Gray has been incarcerated since 1973. Mr. Gray has learned from life, and hard times, and even from love. His artwork reflects all of these.

BIOGRAPHIES

AUTHOR

David Hunter works at Binghamton University, where—among other duties—he serves as a university judicial resolutions officer. He has been involved with community youth court initiatives. In 2004 he returned from the Republic of Kiribati, where he served as a Peace Corps Volunteer for two years. Since that time he has had several articles published in educational magazines.

SERIES CONSULTANT

Dr. Larry E. Sullivan is Associate Dean and Chief Librarian at the John Jay College of Criminal Justice and Professor of Criminal Justice in the doctoral program at the Graduate School and University Center of the City University of New York. He first became involved in the criminal justice system when he worked at the Maryland Penitentiary in Baltimore in the late 1970s. That experience prompted him to write the book *The Prison Reform Movement: Forlorn Hope* (1990; revised edition 2002). His most recent publication is the three-volume *Encyclopedia of Law Enforcement* (2005). He has served on a number of editorial boards, including the *Encyclopedia of Crime and Punishment,* and *Handbook of Transnational Crime and Justice.* At John Jay College, in addition to directing the largest and best criminal justice library in the world, he teaches graduate and doctoral level courses in criminology and corrections. John Jay is the only liberal arts college with a criminal justice focus in the United States. Internationally recognized as a leader in criminal justice education and research, John Jay is also a major training facility for local, state, and federal law enforcement personnel.

INEQUITIES OF THE JUSTICE SYSTEM